GRANDMA U

For Momo and Grandma
—J. R.

To Mom and Blanche (AKA GaGa and Grandma)
Two wonderful grandmothers who inspire us all.
—L. C.

Ω

Published by
PEACHTREE PUBLISHERS, LTD.
1700 Chattahoochee Avenue
Atlanta, Georgia 30318-2112

www.peachtree-online.com

Manufactured in Singapore

Book design by Lucy Corvino and Loraine M. Joyner
Book composition by Melanie M. McMahon
Illustrations created in watercolor and colored pencil

10 9 8 7 6 5 4 3 2 1
First Edition

Library of Congress Cataloging-in-Publication Data

Ransom, Jeanie Franz, 1957-
  Grandma U / written by Jeanie Franz Ransom; illustrated by Lucy Corvino.-- 1st ed.
    p. cm.
Summary: Molly McCool, finding out that she will be a grandmother for the first time, signs up for classes at
Grandma University but doesn't understand when the teacher says the students already know the most
important thing of all.
    ISBN 1-56145-214-9
    [1. Grandmothers--Fiction. 2. Babies--Care--Fiction. 3. Universities and colleges--Fiction.] I. Corvino,
Lucy, ill. II. Title.
    PZ7.R1744 Gr 2002
    [E]--dc21   2002000088

GRANDMA U

Written by
Jeanie Franz Ransom

Illustrated by
Lucy Corvino

PEACHTREE
ATLANTA

When Molly McCool found out she was going to be a grandma, she was worried. I don't know how to be a grandma! she thought.

"Why, I haven't held a baby in years," she told her husband, Frank.

Molly tried to hold her cat, Spike. Spike squirmed out of her arms. He didn't want to be held like a baby.

I don't remember my nursery rhymes, Molly thought. "Was it Jack and Jill who went up the hill?" she asked Frank. "And what were they going for, anyway?"

"I don't remember," said Frank. "And besides, it's not important. I'm going fishing."

"I can't even bake cookies," Molly moaned. "All grandmas know how to do that, don't they?"

Every time Molly baked cookies, they turned out like moon rocks. And they tasted like…. Well, let's just say even Spike wouldn't eat Molly's cookies.

"Want to take some of my cookies with you?" Molly asked her husband.

"No thanks," Frank said with a chuckle. "I don't want to sink the boat."

A few days later, Molly and Frank were bicycling by the local school and saw a big banner over the door.

"Now open!" the sign said. "Grandma University, the school where grandmas learn to be grandmas. Classes start soon."

"That's it!" Molly shouted. "I'm going to Grandma U!" She called the school as soon as she got home.

NOW OPEN ! Grandma University
The school where Grandmas learn to be Grandmas
CLASSES START SOON !

The very next Monday, Molly packed
a lunch, left a plate of cookies for Frank and
Spike, and set off to Grandma University.

Molly's first class was Baby Basics. The teacher, Mrs. Applebee, was a grandmother of six.

THUD! Mrs. Applebee dropped a chubby photo album on her desk. "Care to see a few pictures?" she asked.

While the grandmas OOOHED and AHHHHED, Mrs. Applebee smiled her approval.

"Class, welcome to Grandma University, the school where grandmas learn to be grandmas!" she said. "Some things have changed since you had young children, so you'll probably learn a lot here. You'll even have some fun.

"But remember this...."

Every grandma waited to write down Mrs.
Applebee's next words.

"There's one thing no school can teach you
about being a grandma. It's something you
already know. And it's the most important
thing of all."

Molly raised her hand. "What is it?"
she asked.

Mrs. Applebee smiled. "You'll
learn," she said. "Now let's get down
to business."

What is the most important
thing of all? Molly wondered.

"I know it's been a while since most of you have held a baby," Mrs. Applebee said, "so here are some dolls to practice on. But remember: always keep one hand underneath the baby's neck because the head is very, very wobbly."

Molly picked up her doll. The head fell off. She didn't know whether to laugh or to cry.

Mrs. Applebee rushed over with another doll. "I'm sorry, Molly," she said. "You got my doll by mistake. I usually take the broken one. Here, try again."

Molly picked up the other doll. Nothing fell off. She held the baby doll, thinking of the warm, sweet, snuggly new grandchild she would cuddle in her arms very soon.

"Good job, Molly," said Mrs. Applebee.

I know how to hold a baby, Molly thought. Is that the most important thing of all?

Molly's next class was Bottoms Up.

"There's good news for modern grandmas," said Mrs. Applebee. "Today's diapers are made to throw away. No more washing dirty diapers!"

The grandmas all cheered.

"The bad news is that disposable diapers come in six zillion different sizes and styles—some for boys, some for girls. They all hold as much liquid as Lake Erie. Which means you might not even know the baby's wet…until the diaper explodes. KA-BLAM!"

The grandmas all jumped.

"Now let's do a practice diaper."

Molly raised her hand. "What if you accidentally put a boy diaper on a girl?" she asked.

"As long as you have a diaper on the baby," said Mrs. Applebee, "That's all that matters."

I can diaper a baby, thought Molly. Is that the most important thing of all?

The next class was Gah-Gahs, Goo-Goos, & Giggles.

"First we're going to brush up on our baby talk," said Mrs. Applebee. "Repeat after me... 'I'm going to get those itty bitty toes. Yes, I am, you cutey ootey wootey swe-e-e-tie pumpkin pie!'"

Then Mrs. Applebee gave each grandma a mirror and had them practice making silly faces. "Babies love this," she said.

Molly did, too.

I know how to make babies laugh, Molly thought. Is that the most important thing of all?

"Now we're going to Rock 'n' Read," said Mrs. Applebee. "After we have our peanut-butter-and-jelly lunch, everyone get a book to read. Not just once. Not just twice. You're going to have to read it over and over and *over* again. Sit in a rocking chair if you like."

Molly didn't like rocking chairs. But she did like to read. She collected some pillows and sprawled out on the floor with her book.

"Great, Molly!" Mrs. Applebee said. "Kids love it when you get down on the floor to read. That makes it easier for them to cuddle close to you."

I know how to read to a baby, Molly thought. Is that the most important thing of all?

"Time for recess," said Mrs. Applebee. "Kids love to play, and they want you to play too."

As the grandmas raced to be the first to the playground, Mrs. Applebee shouted, "You all take turns now!"

The grandmas pushed each other on the swings, climbed the monkey bars, and screeched down the slide. (Never climbing back up the slide, of course!)

They played hide-and-seek, catch, hopscotch, and basketball. They even learned how to be soccer grandmas.

I know how to play, Molly thought. Is that the most important thing of all?

After recess it was time for Cyber Grannies.

"Who's ready to touch a mouse?" Mrs. Applebee asked. Some of the grandmas gasped. But Molly didn't. It was just a computer mouse.

By the end of the class, all of the grandmas were exchanging e-mail addresses, surfing the Internet, and designing their own Web pages.

I know about computers, Molly thought. That can't be the most important thing of all.

"Tomorrow we're going on a field trip," said Mrs. Applebee. "Rest up, but don't forget to study your nursery rhymes!"

The field trip was a great success. Molly and the other grandmas went to the park, the zoo, the aquarium, the dinosaur museum, and the ice cream shop—all the places grandkids love to go. On the bus back to Grandma U, all the grannies-to-be sang nursery rhymes at the top of their lungs.

I know how to have fun, Molly thought. Is that the most important thing of all?

Before they got off the bus, Mrs. Applebee announced, "Next time we meet is the class you've all been waiting for—our last class: Crazy about Cookies!"

Everyone cheered, except Molly. I don't know how to bake cookies, at least not cookies that anyone could eat, she worried.

"Bring in your favorite cookies," said Mrs. Applebee. "See you in class!"

The next few days, all Molly could think about was the cookie class. She baked ten different kinds of cookies, but they all turned out like moon rocks. And they tasted like... Well, let's just say that Spike *still* wouldn't eat Molly's cookies.

What if cookie baking is the most important thing of all? Molly thought. She fretted. She fussed. She thought about what Mrs. Applebee had said. Then Molly had an idea.

When Molly got to class on the last day, there sat all
six of Mrs. Applebee's grandchildren.

"The cookie experts," Mrs. Applebee explained.

Oh, no, Molly thought. Real grandchildren. I'll never
pass the cookie test. I'll never be a good grandma.

The children tasted each grandma's cookies.
"Mmmmm," "Yum," and "More!" were all Molly could
hear above the sounds of six munching mouths.

Then the kids saw Molly's cookies.
"My favorites!" said one of the children.
"Mine, too!" said another. And another. And another. And another.
"Those don't look like homemade cookies," grumbled one grandma. And another. And another. And another.
Molly's heart sank.

Mrs. Applebee gave a loud whistle. "Class, I never said you had to bake the cookies. I just said you had to bring them. Grandmas today are often too busy to bake cookies from scratch. And grandkids don't care if you make cookies or buy them. All they care about is spending time with you."

Mrs. Applebee picked up one of Molly's cookies, twisted off the top, and licked off the filling.

"So, go on, every-one," she said. "Go home and be grandmas. And remember: no one ever died from eating a cookie before dinner!"

As the grandmas lined up to leave the classroom, Molly raised her hand.

"But Mrs. Applebee," she said, "what is the most important thing of all?" The other grand-mas nodded.

Mrs. Applebee looked over at her grandchildren and then at the grandmas. She smiled. "You'll know" was all she said.

And not too long after that, Molly finally met the little person she had seen before only in her dreams.

Molly held her new grandbaby. She made silly faces, sang about how Jack and Jill went up the hill to fetch a pail of water, and promised her grandbaby that they'd go to the playground, the toy store, the zoo, even the moon, if that's what they decided to do.

"How I love you, my dear child," Molly whispered.

Was this the most important thing of all?
Somehow she knew it was.